# INSIDE
## MY FEET

# INSIDE MY FEET

## The Story of a Giant

### Richard Kennedy

Illustrations by Ronald Himler

HarperTrophy
*A Division of HarperCollinsPublishers*

INSIDE MY FEET
Text copyright © 1979 by Richard Kennedy
Illustrations copyright © 1979 by Ronald Himler

Library of Congress Cataloging in Publication Data
Kennedy, Richard, 1932–
    Inside my feet.

    SUMMARY: When enchanted boots carry away his father and mother,
a boy tries to find a way to fight the enchantment.
    [1. Giants—Fiction.   2. Fairy tales]   I. Himler,
Ronald.   II. Title.
PZ8.K387In        [Fic]        78-19479
ISBN 0-06-023118-1
ISBN 0-06-03119-X lib. bdg.
ISBN 0-06-440409-9 (pbk.)

First Harper Trophy edition, 1991.

Whatever became of the fifth grade?

Harrisburg, Oregon 1966-67
Dayton, Oregon 1968-69

This book is dedicated to all of you.

# INSIDE
## MY FEET

When I was a child we lived on a lonely road near the edge of a forest where the darkness went in forever like a bottomless lake. Our nearest neighbor was out of sight and sound, and I remember always one night when both my father and mother were carried off down that road into that deep forest. Then I was left alone in the house waiting to be carried off myself. This is the story of that night, which was a bad night, and of the next night, which was worse.

I awoke at midnight as if someone had called my name, but the room was empty and I had not even the vanishing tail of a dream to remind me why I had come awake. I listened deeply. The house and all about was quiet. The steady silence of the moonlight fell on my bed and cast the outline of my window across the floor. Something was strange, but I couldn't sense what it was. Something was wrong, and something was waiting. The seconds counted slowly by like notes in a funeral dirge. I listened and watched the dark corners of my room. Underneath my bed was a large and cold hand that also watched, and waited for me to dangle a naked arm or leg over the side so it could drag me screaming into that dark pit where it would rip and smother me until I was dead, and torment me afterward. But there was nothing unusual in that. It had been waiting since I was five. Something else was waiting . . . some terror unknown to me.

When I was younger I would have got out of bed (careful to avoid the hand) and gone right to my folks' room across the hall, there to climb in bed and lie between the warm mountains of my mother and father, safe in the shadow and small valley of myself. But now I was older, and those easy nights were gone. I must listen and watch alone when the darkness called my name. I could hear my father snoring softly. My mother made a gentle moan.

Leaning forward in my bed, I looked out my upstairs window into the sky, and saw the giant. It was not a real giant, but a giant made up of stars. He stalks across the night sky with bears and dragons and dogs, with gods and goddesses, snakes and goats, and other things that live in the sky. When he was alive he was a great hunter, but now his spirit lives in the heavens. Orion is his name. I knew him best by the belt he wears, clearly made up of three bright stars, the names of which are so ancient that scarcely anyone can pronounce them anymore. This mighty hunter Orion carries a club and a sword and eternally hunts the Milky Way, sinking feetfirst into the western horizon in the early morning. I marked his place in the sky, and so I knew the time. "Just about midnight," I whispered to myself. I settled back into bed, sorry that I had asked. It might have been a better time. Then came the knock from downstairs at our front door.

It was not the clear and candid knock of a visiting neighbor or friend, nor yet the deliberate thumping of a stranger seeking help or direction. Rather, it was a shuffling and uncertain call, as if from a creature who was wounded, or deeply ashamed, a curious sliding and falling away ghost of a knock. But something more was curious as well. Our dog, Harley, had not barked. That was certainly strange. I heard my father get out of bed. I was at my bedroom door across from my folks' room when he came out. He was barefooted, wearing his nightshirt, with a shotgun in his hand. The shotgun was a side-by-side double-barrel 8-gauge with twin triggers. It was our bird gun, but up close it would do for an elephant. It was also used to investigate the rare midnight visitors who came down our road, far past the last humming electric wire. Father carried a lantern in the other hand. He motioned with his head for me to stay where I was. Three steps took him to the head of the stairs. He hesitated, and stepped down. Mother came to the door, pulling on her robe.

Very softly, I said, "Harley didn't bark." She looked at me and nodded, a deep nod descending into old memories and eerie stories I had sometimes heard. Mother had a feeling for these things that father lacked. Father would have said of Harley, "Probably sick." Mother would be more inclined to suggest that he had been changed into a wheelbarrow or something. For father, the world was a straightforward and everyday business until it was proved to be strange or mysterious. As for mother, the world was strange and mysterious until it was proved to be

4

straightforward and everyday business. But more of this later.

A stair creaked and we heard nothing else till the sound of father sliding the bolt on the front door and lifting the latch. For a few moments it was silent. A breath died slowly in my lungs. Then father called up to us.

"Come take a look at this!"

Mother went down first, and I followed in the billow of her robe. Father had moved around a bit and bolted the door by the time we got there. No one else was in the room, and nothing was out of order that we could see. Mother said, "What was it, dear?" Father lifted the lantern slightly, looking past us toward the floor. "They were outside," he said.

I turned and looked. There on the floor were a pair of boots, common in all ways as any honest countryman's boots, except that they were as long as one of my arms, deep enough to hide a bread box in, past all size numbers, boots with leather enough in them to cover a small chair—the boots of a giant! My father rubbed his chin. As I have said, he took strict care of his imagination. He might admit that the weather was strange, but little else. He was a plain man, and reduced the world to the most simple and practical explanations available. Sometimes there is

comfort in that, but it seemed to me completely out of place that he should now say, "Looks like somebody left their boots. Big fellow. I suppose he'll be back for them later." I was relieved, though, that he checked all the window latches before we started back upstairs, and left the room lighted by the lantern he had brought down.

"Harley didn't bark," I said to him. Father stopped with a foot on a step and considered this for a moment.

"Must be sick," he said.

"Or maybe a butter churn," mother muttered. Father raised an eyebrow at her. We went upstairs and got into our beds.

I could hear mother talking to father in the other room. Her remarks—about the boots no doubt, and possibly butter churns—were punctuated by father's agnostic grunts. I bundled a blanket about myself and sat cross-legged on the bed, looking out the window. I couldn't see the front path from that side of the house. I studied the shadow at the east side of the barn. It was a shadow large enough to hide a giant. But nothing moved or glinted there. The star giant Orion walked quietly over my head. My folks stopped talking, yet I knew that my mother was awake and watching and wondering like myself.

I could feel it. And then there came the sound downstairs of someone walking about in boots.

Both mother and father were at their door as quickly as I was at mine. The walking about had been no more than three or four steps, and now had stopped. Father held the shotgun in both hands now, not with a loose strolling bird-hunting grip, but with a hold and touch meant for bear. Whoever it was downstairs, if he wished to remain warm-blooded, would be wise to stand perfectly still for a while longer. Father gave me a stern look and started downstairs. Mother and I waited, and listened.

The next thing we heard was the sound of walking about again. It was not father, but again somebody in boots. And it was not a casual walking about, but a sort of dancing step we heard. This stopped after a few steps and we heard a voice. A flat and weathered voice, not father's voice, a sort of slapping sound that loose bootlaces might make, with a lilting quality about it, almost like singing. But it said little, and as abruptly as it stopped father gave a whoop, and we heard a clatter of something heavy dropped on the floor. Immediately then the boots began stomping and the voice spoke again. The next moment the front door was flung open and banged on its hinges, and at last

Harley began yelping as somebody ran down the front path. Mother and I stumbled down the stairs.

When we ran through the front room we noticed only that father was not there. The door was wide open and Harley was down by the fence barking. We ran down there without even a stick for a weapon, hopping in our bare feet when we stepped on sharp stones. The dog would not go past the fence; a piece of nightshirt was caught on a rail splinter where father had crossed over. We could hear boots running up the roadway, then the crashing of brush, and then it was quiet and cold and we were alone. I looked at mother. Her eyes were intent on the dark road, and the moon lit lines and muscles in her face that I had never noticed before. Harley was whining and looking for solace between our legs. After a minute, mother made a decision. "Back to the house," she said, and we ran back.

On the floor was the shotgun where father had dropped it, or where it had been torn from his hands. Mother bolted the front door and took up the gun. She checked both chambers to make certain it was loaded, then walked around thumping her fist to each window latch to make certain it was closed tight.

"What was it?" I asked. "What happened?"

Mother only shook her head and said, "Upstairs—in my room." I climbed into my folks' bed, on her side, and she sat up in my father's place and leaned the shotgun against the side table. She lit a lamp and sat upright with her arms folded, looking at the door. I lay in the warm and strange smells of the bed and watched her face.

Father could tell stories about winters when it snowed up past the windows, and of yard-long fish he had caught, and how his grandfather had been chased by Indians, and about the time he fell twenty feet out of a tree and wasn't even hurt, and of the birth of twin calves, and that was all exciting, of course. My mother's side of the family was different. Mother knew other kinds of stories. Mother told about a time it snowed *red* snow, and of a fish *her* father caught with a gold watch in it, still ticking, and how her grandfather had returned from woodcutting in the forest with a wound, a deep scar across his forehead, and how ever after he could say only one single word, and only that one word, until the day he died. Unfortunately, mother could not remember what the word was. And she told about the time Cousin Floyd fell out of a tree with a yell, and when those nearby went to help

11

him he was gone and never heard from again, and about the birth of a calf with two heads.

And as mother was full of mystery and dark things, so also was she strangely innocent of the effect of these stories on me. One evening she told me about a dead man that had been found in their root cellar when she was a little girl. He was sitting upright with a half-eaten jar of cherries in his lap. No one knew who he was, or how he had come to be there, or how he had died. "He was as cold as this stone," mother whispered, touching a stone on the fireplace. I wouldn't go to bed that night, and I cried. Mother tried to comfort me. "Just don't think about it, dear," she said. Just don't think about it, dear. . . . Ah, mother! For a long time afterward I kept an eye on that stone, and would not stand or sit within touching distance of it, and feared—as I would fear a dead man—to be in that room alone.

And so whatever this business of the boots was about, it seemed that mother might handle the situation better than father. It was her kind of story. But whatever mother knew, or was considering, she did not tell me. After a while I closed my eyes. Then I slept.

I was awake before the sound of a knock at our door had died in the corners. Mother slid from the bed and took up the lamp. Tucking the stock of the shotgun under her arm, she gave me a cautious look and went out the door. When she was gone into the darkness, I tiptoed to the door and watched the lamplight rolling on the walls as she went down the stairs. Again for a while it was quiet. The light that shone on the stairwell walls was steady now. Mother was at the front door.

"Who is it?" Mother called. "Who's there?" No answer. Mother slipped the bolt and opened the door. In a few seconds she raised her voice to me. "Come," she said. She was bolting the door when I got downstairs. We stood in the light of the lamp, and she pointed toward the floor with the shotgun. "They were on the doorstep," she said. There they were again, the same monstrous boots. Whoever could fit into them could rest his elbow on the eave of our porch. Mother held the shotgun on the boots and walked around them. I noticed she took care not to step on their shadows. Then she got the lamp and looked inside them, nodded, and hummed to herself. Finally she cradled the shotgun in her arm, and said to me, "Did I ever tell you about your Uncle Oscar and that hat he found?"

I shook my head.

"He found it alongside the road, a perfectly

good hat, and he wore it for weeks before he just happened to turn out the hatband one day, and do you know what was inside that hatband?"

"No," I whispered.

Mother nodded wisely. "No one else knows, either, except for your Uncle Oscar. He took the hat and chopped it up into tiny pieces and buried it in the backyard."

I nodded, wide-eyed.

"But he went crazy anyway," said mother. "Come. Upstairs."

"But . . ." I said, hoping she would not leave this crazy mystery of my crazy Uncle Oscar disturbing every hat I should ever after see so that I should ever after be turning out hatbands before I dared to put a hat on my head.

"Never mind," mother said. "Don't think about it. Upstairs now." And we returned to bed.

Mother sat with the shotgun in her lap now, two pillows bunched up at her back, and I lay with my eyes wide open looking at her. Her eyes were set at some far distance, and her expression was grim. How strange, that I had lived with her all my life and I didn't know if she had ever killed anyone. It might be something a son would know about his mother. Perhaps this was not a good time to ask. Her face was as set and

14

steady as an old photograph, and only the flickering light of the table lamp gave it any movement or life. I did not expect that she would make the same mistake as father, whatever that was. Her right thumb stroked the walnut stock of the shotgun, and she watched. We were expecting a visitor.

Twenty minutes passed. Then came a sound from below—the sound of somebody walking about in boots. Yet we had not heard a sound before that, either of the door being opened or the windows being tried. Mother eased out of bed. She was frightened, but at her center she had the fortitude of a hitching post, and her whole courage was summoned up by the time she looked at me and with a shake of her head indicated that I should stay in the room. The walking about had stopped, and mother went out and around the corner. I listened the next few seconds in a silence that could have filled a dozen libraries. Mother had time to reach the bottom of the stairs. I tiptoed out to the hallway again. And then again there came the sound of the boots.

At the very first step I expected the blast of the double-barreled shotgun to announce that my mother had killed someone. But there was no blast, and the sound of the boots was not the

15

apologetic and contrite step of someone caught on the other end of an 8-gauge shotgun. Again it was rather like a dancing step, an irregular hopping step with a sort of rhythm. And when the dancing stopped, there came the same voice as before, chanting or singing a sort of rhyme, though I could not make out the words. Then, "Crash!" I knew that mother had let go the shotgun, and she gave a yell the same as father, and as quick as that the boots began stomping toward the door. The strange voice spoke again, the door was thrown open, and everything went outside.

I ran downstairs. Harley was yelping at someone on the path. "Mother!" I cried. I got the shotgun from where mother had dropped it and hurried down the path. Harley was at the fence, barking up the roadway, but he would not follow. "Mother!" I yelled. I could not see the boots, but I heard them running, well up the roadway. Then they turned in to the woods. I could hear the brush being crushed. Harley was moaning, eager to get back to the house. It was no good trying to get him to go with me up the roadway, and I would not go alone. I stood there for a while in the cold, biting my lip, wondering what to do. At last I fired off both barrels of the shotgun for lack of a better idea, and ran back to the house.

I brought Harley inside with me, since he had been of no use outdoors, and I latched and bolted the door. I took two cartridges from the box on the mantel and loaded the shotgun again. It was yet five hours or so till first light. Weird and uncanny long-dead ancestors from my mother's side of the family whispered in my ear, and I knew what I knew. The boots were coming back for me. Somebody or something meant to carry us all off, and I was next. This was the way things were done. I had heard of such stories. One fine day a family is missed at the Saturday market. A couple of men ride out to see what ails them, and they find only an empty house, perhaps a pot of stew still brewing over the fire, no sign of violence or struggle and not a soul around, and the family is never seen nor heard of again. How long I had I didn't know, but I did not intend to go the same way as father and mother. Now came the practical and shrewd voices of the ancestors from my father's side of the family, and I began to make preparations.

First of all I got more light in the front room—three lamps in all—and I set them around to best light the dark corners. Keeping the shotgun near at hand always, I then got hammer and nails and nailed three large nails into the jamb of the front door and bent them

over with the claw of the hammer. Then I got a ball of twine and, using the nails for eyes, looped three lengths of twine around them and attached the ends to the bolt, the door latch, and the handle. I took the loose ends back to the center of the room and moved a kitchen chair to that spot. Measuring the distance just so, I cut the twine, took the ends in hand, and sat down facing the door. I had built and designed rabbit snares, and this was no more difficult a problem. I tested my work. Pulling on the first length of twine, I slipped the bolt of the door. I pulled the next and the latch lifted. Taking up the shotgun into the crotch of my arm, I pulled the last length of twine and the door swung open. And I had a perfect, clear shot out the door, smack into somebody's oblivion. I rebolted the door and led my twine back to the chair. I was ready. I looked at the clock above the stove. It was nearly 2 A.M. I was wide awake. Harley was already sleeping by the fireplace, although the fire was out. I looked at the door and tried not to think of my mother's side of the family.

The way I had it figured was this: Whoever left the boots was quick to get away before he was caught. Perhaps then he hid around the side of the house, or maybe in the shadow of the barn. Since it took some time to come

19

down from upstairs, it was safe for him to knock as he pleased and then hide. But I intended to catch him on the doorstep this time. At the first knock, before our visitor had a chance to step out of the boots or set them down, I would pull my twine and have the door open on him. And I, a safe distance away, was going to blow him to memories if he made a move to run off. If he wanted to live, he would stand, and he would take me to my mother and father. If I had to kill him, I would go into the forest in the morning alone and track the boots' path and rescue my folks.

An hour passed, but yet I stayed awake. I grew thirsty, but didn't want to leave the chair for a second. Harley grumbled in his sleep. I wondered if this thing wanted our dog, too. And why did it want us, after all? We were simple countryfolk. We had done no one any harm. Well, soon enough I might learn. My turn was coming.

I was just looking away from the clock when the first touch of a knock came at the door. Quickly then, one, two, three . . . the bolt slid, the latch lifted, the door opened, and I was ready. But there was no one there. Harley awoke and started to growl toward the door, but then he stopped and cringed back toward the fireplace. The boots were on the doorstep, sitting . . . waiting. Carefully, I moved to the door, shotgun ready, and looked outside. No one, and no sound at all. I grabbed the boot tops and hefted them inside. I bolted the door, set the boots a fair distance from the chair and studied the situation.

This was very puzzling. How had the visitor gotten away so quickly? The last knock had hardly sounded at the door when I yanked it open. How could he have gotten away so cleanly? Yet there was a greater puzzle to all this. That is, how was he going to get inside the house now? How had he got in the last two times, with the door bolted and the windows locked? I looked at the door and mused on this. Perhaps he had a magnet to move the bolt and latch of the door from the outside. Or perhaps a piece of wire was slipped inside to slide the bolt and lift the latch. Or . . . with an accomplice? Yes, an accomplice—a tiny one, who came down the chimney and opened the door for the giant! I jerked my head to the fireplace in a panic. Not much time had gone since I let the boots in, and I quickly had a fire going in the fireplace. No one would enter that way. It was a comfort to Harley, but not to me. I reconsidered. If someone small had come down the chimney to let in this giant, then there would have been tracks of ashes and soot on the floor. And there were none. No. Whatever it was had to come in by the door.

I turned in my chair away from the boots and faced the door. My attention settled on the bolt. I cocked one hammer of the shotgun. If that bolt moved a hair, we were going to have need of a new door. At this distance the 8-gauge could make sawdust of an outhouse. The fire was welcome, like the touch of a friend at my side. Five minutes slowly passed. I watched that bolt so intently that I could have detected an earthquake in Argentina by its movement. But such a narrow focus of attention is surrounded all about with desolation and weariness, and my imagination drifted. I wondered about Uncle Oscar and the hat. It must have been a piece of paper in the hatband, to lie so flat. What did it say? Or maybe a picture? My eyes burned. I blinked, then closed them for just one moment to refresh them. Two moments passed. Ten passed. I popped my eyes open. I had nearly been asleep. I thumped my head and thrust my back into the chair.

The touch of the fire was now like a full arm thrown about me, and the length of my body was pressed with warmth and comfort. My head jerked back now and then from small ventures into sleep. The shotgun was too heavy to hold up, so I settled the butt of it on the chair between my legs and let the barrel lean on my shoulder, but kept my finger on the trigger. I nodded into sleep, each nod a little longer, each time coming back a little less near the surface of wakefulness, until finally my chin sank on my chest, and so I was asleep.

I slept like a log, but not the whole log. A twig of me was yet awake and taking notice of things. That twig was my finger on the trigger of the shotgun. When the first footstep came to the room I pulled the trigger and blew a hole in the roof large enough to let in the Last Judgment. And the explosion of it, being right below my nodding head, made me kick over backward in the chair and tumble half deafened and stunned onto the floor. Harley was letting out a terrible cry as I scrambled to a wall, shotgun still in hand, ears pounding, eyes blinking, throat full of smoke, expecting any second to be lifted off the ground by the giant and carried stomping out the front door. I rolled twice and turned, getting an elbow under myself, and aimed the gun to where the boots had last been. I had one shot left.

The first thing I could clearly see was Harley, who had now stopped barking and was staring in awe and horror at the boots. Then he retired

under a table to let me carry out my argument with the boots on my own. They were dancing! No one was in them, and they were dancing! I kicked the chair aside to see them better, and glanced at the door. It was closed and bolted. The boots were all by themselves, dancing around in a circle. Well, then, the giant was invisible and could walk through walls. I aimed the shotgun above the boots to about where a giant's stomach would be.

"Stop!" I yelled.

The boots paid no heed to my command, and continued dancing in that circle. I sighted down the barrel of the shotgun. Whatever or whoever was in those boots had just half a second of existence left to them on my schedule, but then the boots, after having danced three times in a circle, *did* stop. I stood up and tried to make out whatever form was standing in them, but it was plain air to me. Then the tongues of the boots began clapping back and forth, and the boots *talked!* This is what they said:

> Inside my bones,
> Inside my meat,
> Inside my heart,
> Inside my FEET!

This little rhyme was so mixed up in its sound with mystery, and time, and memory, and sadness, that I stood listening almost in a trance. But the very last word, FEET, was pronounced with such power and willfulness, that *my* feet responded: *they jumped into the boots!* This was without my will—my feet jumped and took me with them. I had no desire to jump into those boots at all. It was as if a puppeteer's strings were tied to my knees. I could do nothing but obey those invisible sinews of another's will. And my feet jumped with such a force of obedience that I was flung out—back arched, arms thrown wide—and wrenched so suddenly and violently that the shotgun was thrown from my grip. I found myself planted solidly, captured securely in those giant boots. Then I began stomping toward the door!

I should say, rather, that I was *carried* stomping to the door, for I had no control at all in the matter. My knees lifted and my legs moved totally against my will. *This* was how my folks had been carried off, and now I was being carried off myself. In two moments we were at the door, and then I saw the mistake my mother and father had made. If I was to be carried away, the door would first have to be opened. They should never have opened the door, and I determined that rather than let the boots take me outside I would let them bang and beat me against that bolted door until I fell down unconscious or dead. But when we got to the door, the boots stopped, and spoke another rhyme:

> Open wide and you will see
> What shall become of you and me.
> OPEN WIDE!

Now—again against my will—in full obedience to the command of the boots, my hands darted up and I threw the bolt and flung the door open. I could not have done otherwise. Then we ran out and down the pathway. Harley came barking after, of no use for anything *but* barking, and he wasn't sure he wanted to get even that involved.

We ran down the path with great strides. Wherever I was going, it was without a weapon, without even the use of my own feet, perhaps finally without the use of my other parts, even the use of my sense, and I felt if something were not done, and done soon, this would be the doom of us all.

We did not go to the gate, but instead my left boot took a step onto a fence rail, and I flung my right leg over the top. Next, my left leg was flung over, and then I saw the only chance I was going to have. I was hanging on to the fence and the boots were ready to jump to the ground and run up the roadway. But my arms were now in my own power. The boots jumped to the ground just as I wrapped both my arms around the top rail of the fence. I fell forward onto that rail and hugged it as tightly as its bark once had, and my feet turned and twisted as the boots tried to carry me off. I clutched at the fence, stretched out like a night crawler half out of his hole. The boots kicked and clomped, twisted, turned, and in mad, frantic frustration banged me this way and that against the fence, until I was bruised and crying from the pain, holding on for life and in despair that there would be no end to the contest until my arms were torn from my body and I was carried off a horrible broken and bleeding stump to greet my mother and father without even the arms to hug them before we were brought to our end.

Surely that *would* have been the end to the struggle, but there was something in it to my favor. In the violence of their kicking, one of the boots kicked the other boot off, and then, one of my feet being free and under my command, I kicked at the heel of the remaining boot and it dropped to the ground. Exhausted, I let go the

fence and fell into the weeds, but I knew I hadn't but a few seconds and no time to rest, for the boots had stepped up onto the road and were dancing the enchanting circle, and soon they would call for my feet again. I rolled the few feet down the fence line to the gate. The vertical bars of the gate were spaced close together, and I wedged both my feet between two of the bars and turned onto my side, locking my feet into the gate like the turn of a key, holding them there with the whole weight of my body flattened on the gate path. Just then the boots completed the third circle and called out:

> Inside my bones,
> Inside my meat,
> Inside my heart,
> Inside my FEET!

It was two hours at least before sunrise, and longer before I could have any hope of someone passing on the road. I lay there in the gate path, clutching at the gravel until my hands were bleeding, trying to keep my feet tightly locked in the gate as they fought to wrench free and go to the boots, which danced on the roadway in the enslaving circles and many times called that terrible enchantment to my feet. Surely, I thought, my feet would be torn off by this strife and my life's blood spent at that place. But finally the sun rose, and because evil is haunted by the light, the boots ran off down the road and into the dark forest. I saw them go, and remembered no more.

Harley was licking my face and the sun was high when I woke up. My feet were still locked in the fence. I removed myself tenderly and limped back up to the house. My pajamas were torn to rags from writhing in the gravel, and it was all I could do to take care of the animals before I took care of myself. Settling in a tub of water up to my neck, a large kettle close at hand for refreshing the tub, I let the pain soak out and thought about the boots. They would be back, I was sure of it. They were jealous boots, and they had lost their prize. They would be back at midnight.

It was early afternoon yet, and I would have had time to ride to our nearest neighbor and bring grown-up help back with me. Three or four men might be found who would wait with me, grim and ready for the return of the boots. But I concluded that this was not the answer. The boots were enchanted, that much was sure, and enchantments have a wary sort of intelligence. I doubted that the boots would come if anyone but myself alone were in the house. Yes, they would return for me alone, and *only* if I were alone. I was not happy with this conclusion, but I was certain it was so. The coming night's work was up to me. I must allow the boots to come and attempt to take me away into the forest. But this time I was going to be ready for them.

After soaking for an hour in the tub, I doctored my feet with ointments and bandaged them in soft clean linen. I put on slippers then, for my feet were too swollen for my boots, and took the shotgun and Harley with me and limped up to the road. We found the place where the boots had entered the forest. We walked a little way in. Even in the daytime it was dark in there. The trees were set close together and the brush was high. You could not walk fifty feet without offering an ambush to anyone who waited in there. The track of the boots headed straight into the crowding darkness. Harley and I walked a few yards, but stopped while the roadway was yet in sight. I pointed the gun into the sky and shot off both barrels, and listened. The trees muffled even the echo, and there was no other sound from the inner forest. Perhaps my mother and father were already dead. No—but perhaps they were bound and gagged, or too far away to hear. Then let the shotgun blasts be an invitation to the boots, a challenge for them to come and get me this night. Let them come with their strange magic. I would be ready for them with some plain business to kill an enchantment.

Upon returning to the house, I tied Harley to a porch post. I went inside and rigged up a sort of modified rabbit snare with thin wire, cut a hunk of bacon from a side, and went out to the woodpile. I set the bacon and the loop of the snare at a rat's runway under the woodpile, took the other end of the wire and climbed up on top of the wood and lay quiet. Fifteen minutes later I noosed my first rat, a big bold one, and took him inside. I put him in our great iron pot that hung over the fire to cook the huge spicy stews when we had company. I lifted the pot down onto the floor. The rat ran around in the bottom. I left him to meditate on the particular infinity of pot bottoms and went outside to the wood-pile again. It took half an hour to get the second rat, an even larger beast, who snapped and struggled in the noose and looked at me with a cunning and hateful glare. I think he was a general. Into the pot with him also, and then to other business.

I boiled two potatoes with cabbage and ate

that with a hunk of salt beef. It was late afternoon by then. The show would not start until midnight. There was plenty of time yet, so I sat back in father's great stuffed chair to take a nap, and all the dim afternoon until twilight I slept. And I dreamed. I dreamed wild and eerie dreams that ran like knotted rope burning through the crystal hands that hold the sleeping brain, and I awoke with a greater fear of the coming night than I had carried to sleep with me. The sun had set. I got busy with my work.

First I fed Harley and cared for the other animals, then washed the dishes. Since I would be staying downstairs, I lit the fire and stood looking into it for a while, thinking my plan over to discover if there was any fault with it. The rats scurried around in the pot. Probably they were hungry. That was good. Barefoot, for my feet were still too swollen to get into boots, I pulled my chair to my defensive position in front of the door. Next to it I set a small table. Then I gathered my weapons to hand. I got a small sledgehammer and two spikes from the toolbox and set them on the table. Then I went to the pantry for a jar of honey and set it on the table also. It was dark out now. From the mantel, I took the nearly full box of shotgun shells and set them

next to the honey. I went outside and tied Harley to a nearby tree. I didn't want him on the porch to interfere with the boots' arrival. While I was out there, shotgun in hand, I walked down to the fence and took a look up the roadway. Nothing in sight, and no sound. No, not yet. It was too early.

I returned to the house, bolted the door and attached my three pieces of twine as I had the night before, then sat down in my chair. I tested this little invention again, and it worked fine. With rod and rag and oil, I cleaned the shotgun and loaded both barrels. The fire was getting low and I set two large logs into it. Again I sat down, and waited. It was a little after nine o'clock. I was ready, and wide awake.

It was midnight when the boots had come before, and at midnight they would come again. Then I would bring them inside, the same as before. Then they would dance the enchanting dance and say the enchanting rhyme. And then . . . well, we would see what would happen then. I glanced at the table, at the sledgehammer and spikes, the jar of honey and the shotgun shells. Yes, we would see what would happen then. I rubbed the freshly oiled stock of the shotgun and listened to the rats running in the iron pot. The smaller one was trying to go over

the top and kept falling on his back. The general was squealing orders at him. I waited.

The clock above the stove said 10:30 when next I looked. Was it working? Yes, it was ticking. I watched it sleepily. How slowly a clock's minute hand moves. The small brass circus inside the clock seemed weary now after wheeling and swinging and spinning and clicking all day. Quitting time. All the glittering performers that spin the bright rings had gone back to their trucks and trailers and tents, and now only the sluggish caretakers with their brooms and rakes ran the works, pushing slowly around the rings where all day there had been the lively prancing of brass horses with ruby eyes and the tumbling of spring-steel clowns. Would everyone fall dead before midnight, and time come to an end? I shook my head. Oh, oh. What nonsense was I thinking? I was on the edge of sleep. I went to the sink and dashed some water in my face. Eleven o'clock. I wound the clock.

I made a quick trip to the pantry and put some dried apricots on the table. I sat down again and chewed the dried apricots. Good, I was awake again. When the apricots were gone I took a couple of shells from the box and read the printing on the side of them. I kept my eyes away from the clock. Time would go faster that way. Leaning my head back, I looked up through the hole I had blasted in the roof the night before. The great star giant Orion would pass that way soon. I wondered about him, for I knew something of his story. When he lived on earth he was killed by a woman who loved him. But if she loved him, why did she kill him? It didn't make any sense to me. I guess it didn't make any sense to Orion, either, for that great hunter has been hunting among the stars for thousands of years, yet is so vexed and confused by what has happened to him that he is forever stumbling over a small star rabbit and never even notices. My mind wandered on to rabbit snares for a while, and I wondered about rabbit families and what they were like, and if they missed a father or mother rabbit who was snared. While I was pondering this disturbing possibility, the knock came at the door. It was the same scuffling toe-end-of-the-boot knock that I knew well now. I looked at the clock. It was exactly midnight.

Just in case, I cocked both hammers of the shotgun, then with my twine I slid the bolt and opened the door. There were the boots, and otherwise no sight or sound of any living soul, just as I had expected. I gently let down the hammers of the shotgun and walked to the door. Perfectly quiet outside. I could make out the shape of

Harley sleeping by the tree. I took the tops of the boots in one hand, lifted them inside and set them just a short distance away from my fortress chair. After bolting the door again I sat down and studied the boots. The first part of this strange play was done, and in a short while the second act would begin. The boots would dance and call for my feet.

But as the boots sat there before me right then, they were perfectly harmless. I could have stepped into them and out again with no danger. The enchantment, however it was controlled, whatever the terms of its wickedness, abandoned the boots on the doorstep after knocking. Therefore, they appeared as ordinary boots, and although they were extraordinarily large, it was outside the range of a generous-hearted and honest man's intuition that there was anything wrong about them, for the evil had for the moment stepped out. Otherwise, I believe they would never have been brought into a house, certainly not a house where God-fearing folks dwelled. It was only after the boots had gained their entrance, and quiet had settled, that the enchantment would return to work its mischief. My plan was to catch that enchantment and destroy it, to trap it when it returned to the boots, and eliminate it entirely. And so, with the enchantment and its power destroyed, my prayer was that my mother and father would be able to return from the forest.

The evil thing that now waited would come to no door or window, and there was no lock so secure or wall so stout that could keep it away. It would come to the boots out of the very air, collecting itself together like a mist perhaps, as a dank vapor collects in a tomb. It made no sound and had no smell, so Harley knew nothing of it. Even now he slept peacefully. I waited. In a few minutes I began to feel a strange thin presence in the room, an airy and vaporous thing that came in with a chill. It was coming. I laid the shotgun aside and picked up the sledgehammer and the two spikes and waited on the edge of my chair.

Then, with the slightest sucking sound like the last swirl of water going down a drain, the boots came alive with the enchantment and took a step. I waited just a moment, until the second step of the enchanting circle was begun, then I leaped at the boots and in half a dozen blows with the sledgehammer I drove a spike through the toe of each boot, pounding them flat and tight to the floor. I had them! And now they would die! I reached for the jar of honey, unscrewed the lid, crammed my hand inside and smeared great globs of honey all over the boots, inside and out. Then I lugged the great iron pot nearer and with a hard effort lifted it up. As quickly as my strength could manage I tipped it upside down as I brought it banging down over the boots, completely covering them. The rats stayed inside. I put an ear to the pot. The rats were busy already. They were eating the sweet, honey-smeared boots!

And that's that, I thought, as I washed my hands and listened to the rats chewing up the boots. That would be the end of the boots and the enchantment. If my folks did not come back that night, next day I would go into the forest and find them. Even though I feared that, I would have no worry about enchanted boots taking the power of my feet or hands from me. I trusted the shotgun to take care of whatever else was in there. But I could not have used the shotgun to blow up the boots, you understand, because that would only have blasted them to shreds, into so many little enchantments perhaps, and still with power if they could somehow collect themselves together. No. The boots would have to be destroyed entirely, and to be digested in the bellies of two rats would do nicely for that. The only other plan which I had considered was to pour kerosene over them and

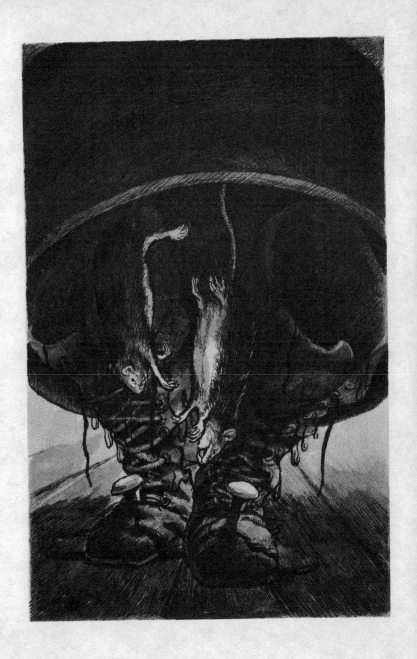

burn them, but I cast off this plan for fear that I might also burn down the house.

The exercise in the pot had been good for the rats' appetites. They ate at the honey-smeared boots for two hours, and they did not stop chewing slowly, as if they were getting full, but stopped suddenly as if there were nothing else left under the pot to eat. I lifted an edge of the pot and rolled it aside. The boots were completely gone. Two spike-heads, shiny from the teeth of the gnawing rats, showed where they had been. But the rats themselves! They were huge! Of course I had expected them to be a great deal fatter from eating the boots, but they had grown entirely and all over, and each was now as long as the boots had been. And they rushed out at me!

I jumped back in alarm, looking for something to leap onto, but before I could get away both rats were at my feet. They weren't biting at me, thank God, for they could have taken my toes off with no trouble, but they began *snuggling* about my feet, *crowding* against my feet, each rat at a different foot, pushing their bristly bodies next to my feet as if they were great hairy slippers that wanted to be put on. Yes—I understood exactly! The enchantment had *not* been destroyed, but had merely entered the bodies of the rats, and they ran in circles around my feet and snuggled as if expecting that I could jump right inside their skins. They squealed all this while, and perhaps it was the enchanting rhyme they were saying, but it had no effect in rat language if it was.

Tripping and stumbling over them, I walked over to the pot. Carefully, ready to snatch back at the slightest show of savagery, I put a hand down to my feet. The rats ignored it. They were interested in my feet only. The enchantment, after all, was not meant to harm me, but only to take me away. I grabbed them both by their necks, lifted them and dumped them into the pot. I had to have some time to think this over. I sat down in my chair. Now what should I do?

Several things were important. For the moment I had the advantage over the enchantment, but that might not last. Dawn and a new day might release greater dangers on myself and the life of my folks, if they were yet alive. The answer I needed had to take advantage of the moment, the imprisonment of the enchantment, and the use of the rats.

The answer that I came up with I did not particularly like, but it seemed the only answer, and time was moving on. Things were going to be much more risky than I had ever figured. I was going to have to enter the forest that night and visit whatever was the master of this magic. But my mother and father were there, and I was going to have to do what I could, although I had barely enough courage to get busy with my next tasks.

Taking up my ball of twine again, I twisted and knotted, and tried out two or three styles until I invented what looked to be a couple of workable rat harnesses. It was fortunate that the rats were harmless, for I could not have managed otherwise. I reached into the pot and slipped both rats into harness, leading the reins over the side of the pot. Once more I checked the shotgun and leaned it against the table. I filled a lantern and fetched a hatchet. Then I put on my jacket and filled a pocket with shotgun shells. That was all I would need for the journey outside. I investigated the rats again. They had tangled the reins of the harness, for they were still running circles, but I soon had that straightened out. I rolled the pot aside and let them out.

They scurried to my feet. With reins held tightly I kept their heads up and forward and stepped onto their broad backs. Their rough hair gave footing to my bare feet, and after a few tries I managed to balance on them. This suited them fine. The enchantment supposed it had captured my feet, although I could step off at any time I chose. I gave the rats their head. They ran to the door and I stayed aboard. They put their noses to the crack, searching for a way to get out. Fine, it was exactly as I figured. The rats would carry me into the forest, and now I had some control. Jerking the reins, I managed to pull the rats from the door. I rode them around the room a few times, turning them this way and that and stopping them at will with a hard pull on the reins. They obeyed me with a grudge, but they did obey me, and in twenty minutes I could ride them as well as I could a goat, which is not easy, but it can be done. So I was ready.

I rode them over to the table and looped the lantern in the crook of my left arm, and in that hand I took up the shotgun. I stuck the hatchet in my belt, took the reins in my right hand and rode the rats to the front door. This was my last chance to give it all up. When I opened that door there would be no going back. I paused a moment. The rats squealed and paced back and forth at the edge of the door. Perhaps the enchantment had some little power left, for although I was very afraid, I was also excited, almost eager to go. And no matter what other danger, my mother and father were somewhere in that forest. All right then. I opened the door, and with shotgun, lantern, hatchet, and a pocket full of shells I rode out barefoot on the boot-fattened rats.

Harley began to bark, and I was glad he was tied up. He would have attacked the rats, putting a quick end to my plan. The rats headed for the fence and would have knocked me silly going underneath it, but I pulled them off their track and to the gate. They could have their own way after we got onto the road. As soon as we were through the gate and on the road I loosed the reins and off we went, the rats full of enchantment under their trembling load. We entered the forest at exactly the place where the boots had entered it on the previous night. The rats dashed into the dark brush. Switching the reins to the hand with the shotgun, I pulled the hatchet from my belt with my other hand. It was a crowded forest, and trees often came within reach. I swung at them with the hatchet as I passed, taking out hunks of bark or scallops off limbs, blazing a trail to find the way back, please God I should ever be coming back.

The brush jabbed and tore at me as we ran on into the darkness, and three times I was knocked off the rats. But I held tightly to the reins, wrapped twice around my fist, and with as much luck as skill I managed to hold the lantern up-

right. It could have broken and slopped me with kerosene, reducing me in a glory of fire to a small heroic handful of cinders with not even a boot nail left to tell the story. Once or twice I fell and was dragged for a few feet by the rats, who seemed nearly crazy with ambition to get wherever we were going and evidently hadn't noticed that I wasn't with them any longer. But I yanked them to a stop and took the opportunity to make some good blazes on nearby trees, for many of my headlong running swings had amounted to no more than thin cuts. Then I mounted my snake-tailed steeds and we were on our way again.

We were perhaps a mile into the forest when the limb of a tree knocked the shotgun out of my hand, and I could not stop the rats to retrieve it. We were nearer the source of the enchantment now, and the furious desire of the rats was growing stronger as we approached that burning center. So I only held on and continued blazing at the trees with the hatchet, concerned now that it should remain sharp at the end of our mad rushing journey, for with the loss of the shotgun it was the only weapon I had left.

How deeply into the woods did we go? I don't know, and no doubt in worry and pain and fear I might have said that the ride lasted for hours, but probably we went no farther into the forest than two miles or so, and I rode the maniac rats for no longer than about forty minutes. I had given up trying to watch ahead by light of the lantern. I held it next to my chest to protect it from being torn from my grip, and the near and bright light of it made the distance even darker. I held my head cocked forward and to the side to save my eyes from being poked out by branches, and gripped the hatchet ready to take a hit at whatever close and solid shape we passed. Sometimes I hit a tree, sometimes not, the wasted effort nearly throwing me from the backs of the rats. If my mother and father had managed to escape and were walking out that way I would probably have taken both their heads off with a single stroke, mistaking them for trees.

Somewhere near the end of our journey my feet began to feel wet. Fearing I was cut badly and bleeding, I bent my knees to investigate. The rats were foaming at the mouth; they turned their red eyes upward to me, weary of the burden and hating it, and yet in their bowels the enchantment burned with the same ferocity and they must go on. They were nearly dead from exhaustion. I pulled them back as much as I could so they would not die on me.

We reached a stream. The sound of the running water was refreshing, and I wished I could go to the edge and wash my wounds, but the rats went directly to a log that stretched to the other side, and we went across. It was difficult footing, and the rats were unsteady. I was nearly pitched over the side but I grabbed a snag to save myself, and in doing so I lost the hatchet. It dropped into the darkness, splashing somewhere below in the stream. I could probably not have found it even in the daylight. Now I had no weapon at all. We gained the other side of the stream safely. The rats were coughing blood. Surely they were near death. They stumbled and lurched, at the end of their strength, the flame of the enchantment almost dead in them except for the bright sparks of their eyes. After leaving the log bridge, I crouched over, coaxing them on, my head close to the heat and fumes of the lantern.

Then, without the slightest notice so that I could prepare myself or give thought or devise a plan, the rats on their last breath crawled into a small clearing and stopped. I looked up. A great bonfire was roaring in the center of the clearing. Off to the side there was a cage made of saplings, in which stood both my mother and my father. My mother was in her nightgown, without her robe, and father was naked. Sitting near the fire on a great log was a barefoot giant. He looked at me with the delight of a spider who has brought a prize to the hot and hungry center of its web, and he roared, "HAH! I THOUGHT THERE WAS ANOTHER ONE!"

At that moment, both rats sniffed, coughed, and died. Feeling a slight sense of pity for them, I slipped from their backs as they rolled over. I dropped the reins and stood staring at the giant, and he at me.

My mother and father cried out to me through the bars of their cage. "Run, run! Save yourself!"

"DON'T SHOUT!" the giant roared at them. He was of awesome size, an old giant with a bald head, although around his ears there were fringes of white hair which hung to his shoulders, and he had a great drooping mustache. He was leaning forward with his forearms resting on his legs. In his right hand he held a needle as long as a bayonet, and in his left hand, smoothed across his knee, was his work. I recognized the material. It was my father's nightshirt and my mother's robe he was sewing at, sewing them together. Then I saw that the giant's jacket was made up of a patchwork of coats, dresses, nightgowns, nightshirts and other such human-sized clothes. Bonfire shadows danced on his face. He smiled a sweet and snaggled smile at me, and

said, only a little softer than when last he had spoken, "IS THAT A WOOL JACKET YOU HAVE ON, BOY?"

He was looking at me past the side of the fire, so he couldn't see that I wasn't standing in his boots.

"Run!" my father shouted. "Run and save yourself!"

"STOP THAT SHOUTING!" the giant roared. He picked up a pair of scissors as long as a sword and snapped them at me. "THESE SCISSORS HAVE SHARP LEGS, BOY. DO YOU WANT THEM TO CHASE YOU?"

I believed that they could, and I had not come that far to run away. I spoke to the giant. "Why have you taken my folks' clothes? What are you going to do to them?"

"WHAT DID YOU SAY?" said the giant, cupping an ear toward me. I repeated my question. "I NEVER COOK ANYONE WITH THEIR CLOTHES ON. THAT'S FOOLISH. WOULD YOU COOK A RABBIT WITHOUT SKINNING IT?"

"Are you going to eat them?" I asked, now noticing forked sticks on each side of the fire, to cradle the spit for roasting meat. "Cook and *eat* them?" I croaked. But of course I knew the answer. The giant was wearing the evidence of his past meals, his coat made of the nightclothes of his victims. I was horrified.

"OF COURSE I'M GOING TO COOK THEM. HOW CAN I

EAT THEM IF I DON'T COOK THEM? I DON'T EAT PEOPLE RAW. I'M NOT A MONSTER, YOU KNOW!"

"But why? What have they done? Why are you going to eat them?" This meant nothing to me, but I was stalling, looking about, trying to think of something to do, some plan, some weapon. . . .

"WHAT?" the giant roared.

I said, "What have they *done*?"

"HOW SHOULD I KNOW WHAT THEY'VE DONE? THEY KNOW WHAT THEY'VE DONE, I DON'T. BUT I EAT EVERYONE WHO CAN'T ANSWER THE QUESTION."

"The question?"

"I WOULD GO HUNGRY AND BE HAPPY IF ANYONE COULD ANSWER THE QUESTION."

"What question is that?" I asked. His needle. If only I could get hold of his needle. But he held it tightly in his fingers, and now he took another stitch at his work and looked up.

"DO YOU WANT TO KNOW THE QUESTION?"

"Yes, if you please."

"WHAT?"

"YES," I yelled. "IF YOU PLEASE."

He looked to his work again. "It's not likely you'd know the answer. Your parents didn't know, either." The giant held his sewing up and shook it out, then smoothed it over his knee again. "Many long times I asked the question of

56

myself, but I couldn't find the answer. I asked and asked and asked, but I got no answer. I decided to see if anyone else could answer the question, so I sent my boots out for them." He squinted at me over the fire. "DO YOU WANT TO KNOW WHAT THE QUESTION IS?"

"Yes, please." I was swinging the lantern from side to side, looking all about the ground near me. A sharp stick might do, even a small club.

"DO YOU WANT TO KNOW WHAT THE QUESTION IS?" repeated the giant.

"YES!" I yelled at him.

"IF YOU KNOW THE ANSWER, I WON'T EAT YOU. WHY ARE YOU SWINGING THAT LANTERN ABOUT?"

"I'm nervous," I said. "I hope you won't eat me."

"That's understandable," said the giant. "Did I ask you if that's a wool jacket? I need more wool for a blanket. It gets cold, and I'm alone."

"Yes," I said. "It is."

"Good," said the giant, taking up his work and examining a hem. Then he went to sewing as if he had forgotten I was there. I was going to have to move from the spot to find a weapon. There was nothing at hand.

"BUT WHAT IS THE QUESTION?" I yelled at him.

"WHAT?" said the giant. "DO YOU HAVE A QUESTION?"

"I was talking about *your* question. The question you ask before you eat me."

"DO YOU WANT TO KNOW WHAT THE QUESTION IS?" asked the giant.

"Please," I said.

"The question is this," said the giant, folding his work and pointing the needle at me. "What became of the child that I was?"

I looked up at him. The giant touched the corner of his eye with the edge of my mother's robe. Then he jammed his needle into the log and glared at me.

"I LOVED THAT CHILD! I NEVER LOVED ANYONE ELSE, BUT I LOVED THAT CHILD. He was gentle, and sweet, and good, and beautiful, and happy. And I don't know what became of him. Nothing has . . . been the same since. I remember how he laughed, and . . ." The giant sniffed and wiped his nose with the robe. "I LOVED HIM."

I looked at my folks. They made a gesture of helplessness. They had no more idea than I did of what became of that child. The giant was caught up in his woe and bewilderment. I watched him, and for a minute forgot my plans for escape in wonder at seeing such a great person cry. He put the palms of his hands to his eyes and smeared at his tears.

"I loved that child so. I loved him," he said

softly. He wiggled his needle loose from the log and spoke in nearly a whisper while he stared closely at its point, as if he were looking at a world vastly faraway in time and place. "The animals came to that child, and he was gentle and kind to them. They ate from his hand, and the birds sat on his shoulders. How I loved him, and even the trees loved him, and all day long there was singing in the wind and water and leaves, and the forest kept him warm and safe, and . . . and . . ."

The giant's eyes were full of tears. After a few melancholy stitches, he turned the needle between his fingers and again dreamed silently of those days. He spoke again. "I remember his face in the water. His eyes. How beautiful. I loved him so . . . his hair, his hands, his mouth. . . ."

A slight motion of my lantern brought him back from this dream and he gazed toward me. I could not help but feel sorry for him. His eyes were full of tears, and he gazed at me out of those dark pools with a deep and kindly sadness from faraway. It was as if he were looking through the past at the very child he had lost, and I felt pity for him and was certain for a moment that this sorrowful and weeping giant would *not* eat us. But then, even as he looked at me, his awareness of the time and place came back to him and I saw his present intentions return to his watery eyes like two water snakes coming to the surface.

"WHAT BECAME OF THAT CHILD?" he roared. Now it was an accusation, as if *I* were at fault for that lost child and deserved to be eaten if I didn't confess at once.

"Did . . . did the child eat people, too?"

"NOT ONE!" said the giant. "Didn't I say he was good and gentle and sweet? Not a bite! He was innocent. It's *ME* who eats people, and I'm going to eat you, too."

"That's a terrible thing to do," I said.

"IT'S NOTHING," said the giant. "What difference does it make? What difference does anything make if you can't answer the question? Who cares? NOW! WHAT BECAME OF THE CHILD THAT I WAS? CAN YOU ANSWER THE QUESTION? I'M HUNGRY."

I looked at my folks again. Father was pointing his finger toward the giant's scissors. They looked too heavy for me to lift. I stalled some more. "So you send the boots out to get people?"

"I taught them everything they know. That poem they say was going around in my head for a long time, and it seemed a good enchantment for boots. Now they go get people for me. Are your trousers wool, too?"

"So you enchanted the boots?" I said. There was a pointed stick lying not far away. It looked like a spit. Ugh! This is what he ran through people to cook them on, I guessed. I wondered if I could lift it.

"I taught them what they say. It's a poem. It rhymes, doesn't it?"

I remembered what the boots chanted after they danced:

> Inside my bones,
> Inside my meat,
> Inside my heart,
> Inside my FEET.

"Yes," I said. "The words 'meat' and 'feet' rhyme. It rhymes perfectly."

"DOES IT RHYME?" the giant roared.

"YES!" I yelled.

"I thought it did," said the giant, patting his work out while he mumbled. "It was just going around in my head like that, and I taught it to the boots. I could have taught them other things. When I was younger I used to write poetry, you know."

"I didn't know," I said.

"I remember my first poem," said the giant. "I cornered a deer and was going to crush his head with my club when I saw it was afraid, and then

I saw a tear in its eye and all at once came the words to my brain: 'fear,' 'deer,' and 'tear.' And I stopped with my club up in the air. I don't know why, just because for a second everything seemed sort of to fit together, you know. Mainly things never seem to fit together. So I sat down and thought of other words to see if anything else fit together, and I wrote my first poem. Do you want to hear it?"

"Of course," I said. And I did. Since I could find no weapon to beat this giant's head with, maybe I could get some advantage by understanding him.

The giant bunched his work in his lap, straightened his shoulders, and recited very like a schoolchild:

> I went out one day to club a deer,
> I found a fat one pretty near,
> Fat and cornered and full of fear.
> I raised my club and then a tear
> Dripped from his eye, and in my ear
> I heard some words and they are here.

After reciting, the giant asked, as if he truly cared for my opinion, "Do you like it?"

"I do," I said, wondering if the giant would let us go if I wept, which I would find easy enough to do. It seemed he might have a soft heart. But immediately he let me know that wasn't the answer.

"You know what's funny," said the giant. "I ran into that same deer the next time I went out clubbing. You know, like there's a kind of magic or something in poetry. So I cornered him again, and I thanked him and told him the poem. He appeared to like it, too. Then I smashed him."

Calmly, the giant took up his sewing again. "I made other poems, too." And he recited again.

> Inside of me a bone man lives,
> His teeth are mine, and mine are his.
> His company is scary, rather,
> But we always eat together.

The giant touched his lip with his needle and mused on this poem. "That's not just right, of course, but I couldn't get it any better. 'Rather' and 'together' don't rhyme perfectly, do they?"

"That's true," I said. "You might have rhymed 'together' with 'weather,' or 'feather,' maybe, but then the whole poem . . ."

"I thought of that," said the giant. "And there's 'heather,' too, and 'leather' . . ."

But then I stopped listening. I *had* it! I had my plan. I had the weapon I was looking for, and poetry had given it to me. Because of this last poem being about teeth, and eating, I remembered the other rhyme the boots had said. There was the little verse they said when they carried me to the door.

> Open wide and you will see
> What shall become of you and me.
> OPEN WIDE!

That was it! Just what I was looking for. "Open wide!" The boots' own words would save us. It was a dangerous plan I had in mind. I was going to have to stand right up in the giant's lap to work it.

The giant was still musing on possible rhymes for "together." "Tether, whether, plether, mether, bether . . . "

"I think I know the answer to the question!" I called to him.

"What question?" Then he remembered his question. "WHAT? NO, YOU DON'T. NO ONE KNOWS THE ANSWER."

"But maybe I do," I said. "I'll have to come over to you to say it. May I?"

"Just come. The boots won't hold you now."

So I pretended to be stepping out of the boots. I walked around the fire and over to the giant. I was no higher than his knee. He put a hand down and fingered the sleeve of my jacket.

"That's good wool," he observed.

"But maybe I know the answer," I said. "And this is what I think. I think maybe I know what became of that child—"

"I loved him," interrupted the giant, and I was afraid he was going to start weeping again.

"I think maybe he's *inside* you," I said.

"Huh?" grunted the giant. "How can that be?"

"Let me show you," I said. "Let me climb up on your knee."

The giant grabbed me by the back of the coat and lifted me like a kitten. He set me on his knee.

"If that child is inside you," I said, "then I can look down your throat and see if he's down there."

"HOW WOULD HE GET INSIDE ME?" the giant yelled in my face. "I NEVER ATE HIM."

"I don't know. Maybe it's a mystery. But bend down and I'll look."

"All right," said the giant, and he lowered his head a bit.

"Open wide!" I said, using his own enchanted words against him. And he opened his mouth wide.

I grabbed his mustache for a handhold and looked up his hairy nostrils. On the walk around the fire I had loosened and flipped off the cap of the kerosene well of the lantern. If the giant had had more teeth the plan would not have worked. But there was just room, and I shoved the whole lantern sideways into the giant's mouth! He lurched backward. I held tight to his mustache, wrapped my legs around his neck and reached into my pocket. I grabbed a handful of shotgun shells and threw them in after the lantern. Then I fell clear of the giant as he tumbled backward off the log gagging on the half-swallowed lantern and shotgun shells, then he belched and a roar of fire bellowed out of his mouth. He choked out screams and clutched at his throat, stumbled to his feet and ran off into the darkness, his mustache afire and streaming sparks behind him. Roaring like an open furnace he ran through the trees.

"He's headed for the stream!" my father cried. "The scissors, quick!"

That was my idea exactly. I dragged them over to the cage and father took them from the inside and worked against the vines that tied the bars together. Two of the bars fell, and my folks were free. "This way," I said. "I blazed a trail."

"My nightshirt," said father, who was still naked.

"No time," mother said. I took off my jacket

and father tied the arms around in back of him. It fell in front like an apron. Then I ran back around the fire. My folks were close behind. I found the dead rats, and headed into the forest at that spot. We had run only a few seconds when there came a great explosion behind us. The fire had gotten to the shotgun shells.

"He didn't make it," said father. "He exploded."

"It's about time," said mother.

We hunted the trees for my hatchet marks. Smaller explosions came from behind us as we ran on. We crossed the stream, which must have curved around to where the giant had run off. It was still dark, and we found as many blazes by feel as by sight. Behind us, all was quiet. We moved very slowly so we would not get lost, and I told my folks how I had saved myself on the fence, and how the rats had eaten the boots and that I had trained them and ridden them into the forest.

"Good boy," father kept saying. "Good boy."

We groped at the trees in the dark for a long while. The sun was just coming up when we found our way past my last tree blaze and out of the forest. We mounted the roadway and headed toward the house. Harley began barking as we came in the gate. And then we were home.

Mother and father stayed up, but I went to bed. I lay there stunned with tiredness and could not sleep. I thought of what I had done to the giant, and I was bothered. My folks came in. Mother had some hot chocolate for me. Father sat down and put his hand on my shoulder.

"I'm sorry about the giant," I said. "I don't like what happened to him."

"You had to do it," said father. "It was a brave thing, and you know how he was."

"But he was so sad about that lost child. I felt sorry for him."

"You did right," said father. "That was a good plan."

"He liked poetry, too. The deer poem was nice."

"Remember what happened to the deer," father said.

"I don't feel good about it," I said, and took a sip from the cup. "I didn't know that giants cried." Father patted my shoulder and nodded.

"Giants cry," he said.

"He was so sad," I said.

"That's no excuse for eating people," father said. He touched my head and stood up.

Mother kissed me on my temple. "Just pretend it didn't happen, dear."

Ah, mother.

"Sleep well, dear," she said, and they went downstairs.

I looked out the window. The great star giant Orion had long ago stepped below the horizon, and for a weary while before I slept I lay looking out at the coming day, and wondered what was going to become of the child that I was.